little grasshopper books™

Mother Goose Rhymes

Get the App!

1. Download the Little Grasshopper Library App* from the App Store or Google Play. Find direct links to store locations at **www.littlegrasshopperbooks.com**

2. Wait for the app to Install and open it.

3. Tap the **+ Add Book** button at the bottom of the screen.**

4. Line up the QR Code Scanner with the QR Code found below.

5. Your book will automatically start downloading to your app!

6. Be sure to accept any prompts that come up.

7. Information on device compatibility and troubleshooting can be found at **www.littlegrasshopperbooks.com**

Based on the classic rhymes; illustrated by Stacy Peterson.
App content developed in partnership with Filament Games.

ISBN: 978-1-64030-902-9
Manufactured in China.
8 7 6 5 4 3 2 1

*We reserve the right to terminate the apps.
**Smartphone not included. Standard data rates may apply to download. Once the app and an individual book's content are downloaded, the app does not use data or require Wi-Fi access.

Little Boy Blue
Little Boy Blue, come blow your horn!
The sheep's in the meadow, the cow's in the corn.
Where's the little boy that looks after the sheep?
Under the haystack, fast asleep.

The Robin

A robin and a robin's son
Once went to town to buy a bun.
They couldn't decide on plum or plain,
And so they went back home again.

Miss Muffet

Little Miss Muffet
Sat on a tuffet,
Eating of curds and whey.
There came a big spider,
Who sat down beside her,
And frightened Miss Muffet away.

The Cat and the Fiddle
Hey, diddle, diddle!
The cat and the fiddle,
The cow jumped over the moon.

The little dog laughed
To see such sport,
And the dish ran away
With the spoon.

One, Two, Buckle My Shoe

One, two,
Buckle my shoe.

Three, four,
Knock at the door.

Five, six,
Pick up sticks.

Seven, eight,
Lay them straight.

Nine, ten,
A good, fat hen.

Wee Willie Winkie

Wee Willie Winkie
Runs through the town,
Upstairs and downstairs,
In his nightgown.

Rapping at the window,
Crying through the lock,
"Are the children in bed?
Now it's eight o'clock."

Little Jack Horner

Little Jack Horner
Sat in the corner,
Eating a delicious pie.
He put in his thumb,
And pulled out a plum,
And said, "What a good boy am I!"

The Mouse and the Clock

Hickory, dickory, dock!
The mouse ran up the clock!
The clock struck one,
The mouse ran down,
Hickory, dickory, dock!

Mary, Mary, Quite Contrary

Mary, Mary, quite contrary,
How does your garden grow?
With silver bells and cockle-shells,
And pretty maids all in a row.

Baa, Baa, Black Sheep

Baa, baa, black sheep,
Have you any wool?
Yes sir, yes sir, three bags full.
One for the mister,
And one for the dame,
And one for the little boy
Who lives down the lane.

Pat-A-Cake

Pat-a-cake, pat-a-cake, baker's man.
Bake me a cake as fast as you can.

Pat it, and shape it, and mark it with "B",
And put it in the oven for Baby and me!

Humpty Dumpty
Humpty Dumpty
Sat on a wall,
Humpty Dumpty
Had a great fall.

All the King's horses,
And all the King's men
Cannot put Humpty
Together again.

Sleep, Baby, Sleep

Sleep, baby, sleep,
Your father tends the sheep.
Your mother shakes the dreamland tree,
And from it fall sweet dreams for thee.
Sleep, baby, sleep.